T0130389

Space Dreams

Cynthia Vawter

AuthorHouse™
1663 Liberty Drive
Bloomington, IN 47403
www.authorhouse.com
Phone: 833-262-8899

Because of the dynamic nature of the Internet, any web addresses or links contained in this book may have changed since publication and may no longer be valid. The views expressed in this work are solely those of the author and do not necessarily reflect the views of the publisher, and the publisher hereby disclaims any responsibility for them.

Any people depicted in stock imagery provided by Getty Images are models, and such images are being used for illustrative purposes only. Certain stock imagery © Getty Images.

This book is printed on acid-free paper.

ISBN: 978-1-6655-5123-6(sc)
ISBN: 978-1-6655-5124-3(e)

Print information available on the last page.

Published by AuthorHouse 02/11/2022

authorHOUSE®

Space Dreams

Written and illustrated by Cynthia Vawter

"But Dad, I'm not tired! Can't I stay up a little while longer?" "Not tonight Brandy, just close your eyes and you'll be asleep in no time" responded Dad.

Hmmmp! Parents think they know everything! "Just close your eyes" he says. They are closed as tight as I can get them and I still can't sleep! Shows how much he knows, I thought, as I lay there tossing and turning.

Welp, here I am still awake. It'll be time to get up for school before I know it. Oh well, I can't wait for science anyway because Mrs. Vawter has been teaching us all about the solar system. I wonder what she will talk about tomorrow? Today she said the sun is really just an ordinary star and that it is the center of our whole universe.

I wonder....if the Sun is the center of the whole universe, then, I bet if I went there that I, too, could become so very famous and would be the center of all the attention. Oh yes! I so love everyone making a fuss over me! It is decided! I will go to the sun! I will be the largest star of them all!

So, I sat up in my bed and made a wish on the very first star I saw. "Star light, star bright, first star I see tonight. I wish I may, I wish I might, travel throughout the sky tonight!"

Great day in the morning! Look at me! I'm heading for the sun straight to stardom! I set the spaceship on automatic pilot and began thinking about which planet I would visit after conquering the sun. Perhaps I shall do a little sightseeing on the planet Mercur......

Oh noooooo!!!!!!!!! It... it... it's too hot!!! I've got to turn this baby around before I get toasted! Grunt! Uhhhhh! I... I... can't... yes... yes I can! Mrs. Vawter says "never say can't!" Phew! I made it, just in the nick of time! Goodbye stardom! I just can't take the heat!

Hmmmm. Maybe I will be far enough from the sun's heat on the planet Venus. After all, it's the second planet from the sun. Wow! It looks almost as big as the planet Earth! It is so beautiful and bright! Mrs. Vawter said it had the nickname of Evening Star. I guess this is why. Uh oh. She also said that although it appears to be fabulous that it is covered with thick, poisonous clouds. This is not the planet for me either! See ya!

Phew! Mercury doesn't look too happenin' from here! There are rocks and craters everywhere! No trees or grass in sight. It actually resembles a lot of the pictures of the Moon that I have seen before. Gosh, I don't see any rivers, lakes or oceans either. How could I survive here? I don't think that this is the right planet for me. Phew! It's too close to the Sun too! It's hotter than an egg frying in a pan. Toodles!

Well, maybe I should consider the moon. After all, people have already walked on the moon. Look! There is the flag that the astronauts left. I don't know about this either. Mrs. Vawter told us that it doesn't have any air, water, plants or animals. Sounds kind of boring to me. However, because it doesn't have any gravity, I sure could do some great cheerleading jumps!

"Yo! Brandy! I think it's time for you to be getting home now. You can visit other planets and stars another night" said the Man in the Moon. So, off I went soaring through space back to planet Earth. I just couldn't wait to tell Mrs. Vawter and all the kids at school about my visit in space.

The End

Printed in the United States
by Baker & Taylor Publisher Services